The
Goose Girl

Other brilliant stories to collect:

The Goose Girl

Retold by
Gillian Cross

Illustrated by
Jason Cockcroft

📖 SCHOLASTIC
Home of the Story

Scholastic Children's Books,
Commonwealth House, 1–19 New Oxford Street,
London WC1A 1NU, UK
a division of Scholastic Ltd
London ~ New York ~ Toronto ~ Sydney ~ Auckland
Mexico City ~ New Delhi ~ Hong Kong

First published by Scholastic Ltd, 1998

ISBN 0 590 54384 9

Printed by Cox and Wyman Ltd, Reading, Berks.

6 8 10 9 7

To Sébastien Daniell

Once there was a princess whose father was dead. She was promised in marriage to a king's son in a distant country, but she stayed in her mother's house until she was old enough to be a wife.

While she was growing up, her mother, the queen, collected a great

store of treasure to go with her. There were rubies and diamonds and sapphires; necklaces of river pearls and goblets of golden filigree; rolls of Chinese silk and carpets from the desert.

But the greatest treasure of all was a horse called Falada. He was a handsome and noble horse and, when the time was right, he could speak.

At last, the princess was old enough to leave and travel to her husband's country. Before she went, her mother called her in.

"I've given you many treasures to take with you," the old queen said. "But before you leave I'm going to give you one more thing, to protect you on your travels."

She called to her maid in waiting.

"Bring me a white linen cloth."

The maid brought the cloth and the queen took a needle and pricked her own finger until it bled. Holding her hand over the linen cloth, she let the

blood drip, so that the white cloth was stained with three red drops.

"Keep this safe," she said to her daughter, "and nothing evil will be able to touch you."

The princess took the cloth and hid it inside the front of her dress. Then she put on a rich travelling cloak and covered her face with a silk veil.

"Put on *your* cloak too," the queen said to her maid. "You're going with my daughter, to be her companion and carry her gold cup."

The maid put on her rough woollen cloak and her shabby white veil and

followed the princess down to the courtyard. There was a train of pack-horses waiting there, loaded with treasure. And beside them was Falada, saddled up for the princess to ride.

"Fetch another horse for my maid," the queen called to the stable boys. "She's going to travel with the princess."

The stable boys thought it was a pity to send away another good horse, so they fetched a bony, broken-winded gelding from the stables and gave him to the maid.

When she and the princess had
mounted, the queen said goodbye to
her daughter and the two young
women set off for the distant country
where the prince lived.

They had not travelled very far when
the princess began to feel thirsty, so
she turned off the track and rode down
into the trees beside the river. The
maid followed, on her ugly old horse.

"Please get down," said the princess, "and fetch me some water in my gold cup. I'm very thirsty."

Why should I do what she says? thought the maid. *There's no one to make me obey.*

So she said, "Get down yourself if you want some water, and drink without your gold cup. I'm not going to be your slave."

The princess was upset, but she saw that the maid was fierce and determined. *We have a long way to travel together*, she thought. *It's better not to quarrel.*

She slid off Falada's back and knelt down by the river, trying to look as though she didn't care. But as she stooped over to drink, she started to cry.

The three drops of blood heard her, and spoke from where she had them hidden.

"If your mother saw you now, it would break her heart."

The maid looked down from her horse and thought, *If it were not for those three drops of blood, I could overpower this princess and have what I long for.* But she knew the power of the linen

cloth, and she didn't dare to touch the princess.

The princess mounted and they travelled on, but before long she was thirsty again and she rode down to the river, with the maid close behind her.

"Please get down," said the princess, "and fetch me some water in my gold cup. I'm so thirsty I shall die if I don't

have a drink."

"Why should I get down?" said the maid. "There's water in the river. Go and drink it, if you're thirsty."

So, for a second time, the princess dismounted from Falada and went down to the river, struggling to hide her tears. But she couldn't hide them from the drops of blood on the linen cloth.

They spoke to her again. "If your mother saw you now, it would break her heart."

The maid heard them and scowled, thinking of what she longed to do. But

she didn't dare to try.

Then, as the princess stooped over the river to drink, the linen cloth fell out of her dress. It floated away down the river, and was lost for ever.

The princess didn't see it fall, because she was stooping, but the maid saw, and her heart leapt. *My moment has come!* she thought. *The princess has lost the three drops of blood and now she will be too weak to defend herself.*

She slid quietly off her horse, and pulled a dagger out of her belt. Creeping up behind the princess, she

caught hold of her long, golden hair and held the dagger to her throat.

"Take off all your fine clothes," she hissed, "and give them to me! Or I will kill you and throw you in the river."

When the princess felt the knife blade against her throat, she knew it was useless to struggle. She stripped off her rich cloak and her silk veil, and all

her beautiful wedding garments.

"Take my old grey dress," said the maid, "and my cloak and veil. You must wear those now."

So the two of them changed clothes in the trees by the river, with no one but the horses to see. Falada watched it all, but he did not speak.

When the maid was dressed in finery and draped with jewels, she pressed the point of the dagger against the princess's ribs.

"Now swear that you will never tell anyone what has happened here," she said. "If you don't swear, I'll stick this

dagger into your heart and leave you for the wolves to eat."

The princess saw that she meant it, and she was very frightened. "I swear that I will never tell a living soul," she said.

The maid was triumphant. "Now I am the mistress! And I shall be the prince's bride! You are the maid, and you can ride that ugly old horse. Falada is mine."

Putting her foot in the stirrup, she jumped into the saddle and stuck her spurs into Falada's sides. The princess mounted the old horse and followed

her, and that was how they travelled
on to their destination.

At last they reached the country
where the prince's father ruled. When
they rode into the city, people ran
along after them, shouting and cheer-
ing. The maid went haughtily
through the crowds, but the princess
rode with her head down and her eyes

on the ground.

They passed under a great arched gateway and clattered into the court-yard of the old king's castle. The prince hurried out to meet them. Seeing the maid, in her rich clothes, he thought that she was his promised bride, and he greeted her joyfully.

"Welcome to your new home!"

He did not even notice the shabby princess, who dismounted to hold the horses. He was longing to hear the voice of his bride. But all he got was a haughty nod as he lifted the maid down from her saddle.

The prince was disappointed, but he did not let it show. *She is tired*, he thought, *after her long journey*. Gently he took her hand.

"Come into the great tower," he said. "The king my father is waiting to meet you."

The princess was left in the court-yard, holding the horses, while the maid swept off on the prince's arm. Falada saw it all, but still he did not speak.

Up in the tower, the old king was looking down at the courtyard. He saw the princess, and she looked so humble and gentle that he wondered who she was.

"Tell me," he said to the maid, when the prince had presented her, "who is that young woman holding the horses?"

The maid tossed her head. "She's

not worthy of your notice, sire. She's a poor, ignorant girl who came to keep me company on the journey. Now that we're here, she needs some work to do, or she'll lounge around being a nuisance. Can you find her a job?"

Just at that moment, there was a loud noise of hissing and honking. A great flock of geese came under the arch and into the yard. They scattered everywhere, pecking at the servants' legs and annoying the horses. Running behind them was a boy in a feathered hat. He tried to round up the geese, but there were

too many of them.

"Poor Conrad," said the king. "He has to drive those geese to the meadows every morning and bring them back at night, but he finds it hard to control them. The girl in the courtyard can help him."

"Excellent," said the maid. "It will suit her very well to be a goose girl."

She curtsied and went off with the prince, to see the apartments set aside for her. They were beautiful rooms, with carved furniture and embroidered hangings. When she saw them, the maid was even more determined

to keep the princess's place.

But through the window she caught sight of the horses in the courtyard. And she remembered that Falada could speak, when the time was right.

Who knows when that will be? she thought. *If he tells what he saw in the trees by the river, I shall lose everything.*

Turning round, she gave the prince a false, wheedling smile. "Will you do me a favour?" she said. "To celebrate our meeting."

"Anything you like," said the prince.

The maid pointed through the

29

window. "Do you see those horses in the courtyard? The big horse looks noble and handsome, but he's a foul, ill-tempered brute. I rode him on my journey here, and he threw me to the ground three times. Please send him to the knacker's to be killed, so he can't give me any more trouble."

The prince had not expected anything like that, and he was upset by the idea of killing such a fine-looking horse. But he would not break his promise. Calling a servant, he gave orders that Falada should go to the knacker's.

Immediately, the servant went down to the courtyard and took charge of both the horses. The princess thought they were going to be fed and groomed, so she handed them over gladly. But only the ugly old gelding went to the stables. Falada was led off to the knacker's, straight away. And still he did not speak.

By the time the maid sat down to dinner, he was dead.

When the princess found out what had happened, she felt that her heart would break. *My only friend has gone,* she thought. *Falada was the only one who knew about me.*

She couldn't bear to be so alone. That night she took the few gold coins she had in her purse and slipped out of the castle. Going under the great arched gateway, she crept down to the lower part of the city and went to visit the knacker's man.

"Today you killed a fine horse from the castle," she said. "If I give you this gold, will you nail up his head in

the arch of the great gateway?"

She knew she would walk under that arch every day now that she was a goose girl. That was the way Conrad drove the geese out to the meadows.

The knacker's man thought it was a strange request, but he promised to do as she asked. The princess gave him the gold and crept back to the castle.

Next morning, as the sun was coming up, she and Conrad set out for the meadows, driving the geese between them. As they passed under the great dark gateway, the princess looked up into the shadows, high above. There was Falada's head nailed to the wall.

She nearly fainted with grief. With tears running down her face, she called up to him.

"Falada, O alas, alas,
That you should hang there as I pass."

Then, at last, Falada spoke. From

the darkness, a faint voice drifted down as the head answered her.

> *"And O alas, alas, Princess*
> *That you should pass in such distress."*

Then the geese hissed and Conrad shouted, and the princess walked on under the archway.

When they reached the meadows, the geese wandered about to feed on the grass. Sitting down on a stone, the princess untied her hair, so that she could comb it. As she shook it out the sun caught it, and Conrad saw that it was pure gold.

I want some of that golden hair, he thought.

He was sure the princess would never give him any, so he waited until she started combing it and singing to herself. Then he crept up behind her. He was planning to snatch a hair before she could stop him.

But the princess saw his shadow creeping up on her and she changed her song. Pulling the comb through her hair, she sang to the wind:

"Blow wind
over stone
for a princess all alone.
Blow wind
over water
to protect a queen's daughter.
Blow wind
wild and free
to keep harm far from me."

Immediately, there was a great gust of wind. Conrad's feathered hat was snatched off his head and it went tumbling over the grass. He ran after it as fast as he could, but the wind blew it here and there all around the meadows.

By the time he caught it, the princess had plaited her hair tightly and pinned it close to her head, and he had no chance of stealing even a single hair.

He was so angry that he sulked all day and refused to speak to her.

The next day, they walked out with the geese again, and when the princess went under the archway and saw Falada's head she called up to him again.

"*Falada, O alas, alas,*
That you should hang there as I pass."

Again the head answered her from high in the shadows and Conrad heard

it and sulked, kicking at the cobbles.

When they reached the meadows, Conrad wandered off. He pretended to look at the geese, but really he was waiting for the princess to take out her comb. When she untied her hair, he started sneaking up behind her. This time, he was determined to steal a golden hair.

But the princess heard his footsteps in the grass. Pulling the comb through her hair, she sang to the wind again:

"Blow wind
over stone

for a princess all alone.
Blow wind
over water
to protect a queen's daughter.
Blow wind
wild and free,
to keep harm far from me.

The moment she finished singing, the wind blew out of nowhere, twitching Conrad's hat away. It went spinning towards the river and he had to run hard to save it from falling into the water.

When he came back, the princess's

hair was twisted close to her head and fixed with combs and pins. Conrad was too angry to speak. He stumped up and down the meadows, working out how to get his revenge.

When they returned to the castle, he demanded to see the king.

"Sire," he said, "you must take away that girl you sent to herd the geese with me. I can't work with her."

The old king was amazed. "Why not? She looks gentle and quiet enough."

"She is not gentle or quiet," Conrad said. "She is strange and troublesome. When we go out in the morning, she talks to the horse's head that is nailed up in the great archway. And the head talks back to her."

That sounded more than strange to the king and he began to wonder about the goose girl. "Is that all she does?"

"No, it isn't," said Conrad. "When we're in the meadows, she sings to the

wind. And the wind blows my hat away."

That sounded even stranger. The king decided that he had to see these things for himself.

"Put up with the girl for one more day," he said. "If you still complain after that, I will find her some other work."

Grudgingly, Conrad agreed.

In the morning, he and the princess set out again with the geese. But this time the old king was behind, following them secretly. As they walked under the great gateway, he saw the goose girl look up into the shadows, high above. And he heard her say:

"Falada, O alas, alas,
That you should hang there as I pass."

From out of the darkness came an answering voice that made the king's hair stand on end.

"*And O alas, alas, Princess*
That you should pass in such distress."

This is even stranger than I was told,
thought the king. And he crept on
behind the geese.

When they reached the meadows, the
princess loosened her hair and began
to comb it. The king saw that her hair

was all of gold, and he saw Conrad creeping up behind her, to steal a hair. But before he was near enough to snatch at one, the princess felt the grass rustle, and she started to sing.

At the sound of her voice, the wind began to blow. In a moment, Conrad's hat was tweaked off his head and it went sailing across the meadow and out on to the river. Conrad had to wade in, up to his knees, to get it back.

The old king watched the goose girl plaiting her hair and pinning it round her head. *She is a good, modest girl*, he thought, *but there is a mystery here.*

When the geese came back in the evening, the king sent a servant to fetch the goose girl. She came in her shabby old clothes, for she had no others.

"I saw two strange things today," said the king. "First, I saw you talk to a horse's head in the archway, and I heard it answer you. Then, when you sang in the meadows, the wind came from nowhere and blew off Conrad's

hat. Tell me who you are, and why the horse's head called you 'Princess'."

"I'm sorry, sire," said the princess, "but I can't tell you that."

"I am the king, and I command you to tell me!"

"I can't," the princess said. "I swore a solemn oath never to tell the story to anyone."

"You *shall* tell me! If you don't, I will have you beaten and locked up!"

The princess began to cry, but she wouldn't break her promise, even though the king threatened her with worse punishments, to test her.

When he saw how true and faithful she was, he liked her even better than before. "Don't cry, my dear," he said. "I won't make you break your oath. But I can see that you want to tell the secret."

"Indeed I do!" the princess cried. "But I can never tell you, or any living soul, for that is what I swore."

Then the king saw a way to rescue her from her oath, without forcing her to break it. He pointed to the great iron stove in the corner of the room. In winter, huge logs were burnt inside it, but now it was empty for the summer.

"Creep in there," he said, "and tell your secret to the stove. That isn't a living soul."

The princess crept into the stove and pulled the door shut behind her. Then she started to wail and cry.

"Alas," she said. "If my mother the queen could see me now, she would die of grief. She sent me here to be the

prince's wife, but my wicked maid forced me to change clothes with her. Now she is the bride and I am only the goose girl. Alas, alas!"

As she spoke, her voice boomed and echoed inside the iron stove. The king heard every word.

He sent a servant to find the prince and then he opened the door of the stove and called to the princess.

"Come out, my dear, and let me talk to you."

He and the prince asked her complicated questions about her family, and about the country where she was

born, and she answered every one.

When they saw that she was indeed the true bride, the king was delighted. And the prince wept for joy to find that his wife was this humble, gentle girl, and not the arrogant and overbearing maid.

"Tonight," said the king, "there is a great feast to celebrate the wedding. By the end of the feast, you will have

your rightful place. And the false bride will have chosen her own punishment."

Then the princess was given splendid clothes and jewels, and a place was set for her at the wedding feast. The maid was at the feast too, sitting at the high table, next to the prince, but she was so proud and haughty that she did not once look at the modest princess.

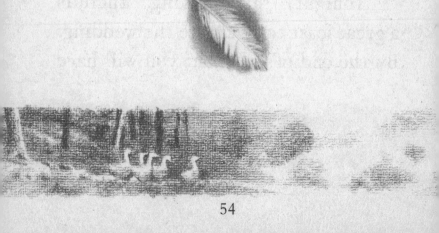

When the feast was nearly over, the old king spoke to the false bride. "I have to judge the case of a disloyal servant," he said. "Instead of looking after her mistress, she threatened to kill her, and stole all her possessions. How do you think I should punish someone like that?"

The maid was flattered that he asked her opinion. "A treacherous servant deserves the worst punishment," she said grandly. "This woman should be shut into a barrel full of nails and dragged through the streets by horses, until she is dead!"

The king stood up. "You shall have your wish!" he said, in a terrible voice. "For you are that servant, and here is the mistress you betrayed!"

Stepping down into the hall, he went to the true princess and took her hand. "Come up to your rightful place," he said. "You are the prince's real wife. The false bride shall have the punishment she chose."

The guards dragged the maid away to meet her fate and the princess stepped on to the dais to take her place beside the prince. He loved her twice as much because she had once

been a goose girl, and so they cele-
brated their marriage, and lived hap-
pily ever after.

Other stories to collect:

Aesop's Fables

Malorie Blackman

Illustrated by Patrice Aggs

Once upon a time there was a man named Aesop
who told stories full of wisdom…

Hansel and Gretel

Henrietta Branford

Illustrated by Lesley Harker

Once upon a time there were a brother and sister
who were left alone in the forest…

The Snow Queen

Berlie Doherty

Illustrated by Siân Bailey

Once upon a time there was a little boy whose
heart was turned to ice...

The Twelve
Dancing Princesses

Anne Fine

Illustrated by Debi Gliori

Once upon a time there were twelve princesses,
and no one knew why their shoes were full
of holes...

Grey Wolf, Prince Jack and the Firebird

Alan Garner

Illustrated by James Mayhew

Once upon a time there was a prince who set out
to seek the mysterious firebird...

Mossycoat

Philip Pullman

Illustrated by Peter Bailey

Once upon a time there was a beautiful girl whose
mother made her a magical, mossy coat...

The Six Swan Brothers

Adèle Geras

Illustrated by Ian Beck

Once upon a time there was a brave princess
who saw her six brothers turned into swans...

The Seal Hunter

Tony Mitton

Illustrated by Nick Maland

Once upon a time there was a cruel fisherman
who was dragged to the bottom of the ocean
by a seal prince...

Cockadoodle-doo, Mr Sultana!

Michael Morpurgo
Illustrated by Michael Foreman

Once upon a time there was a rich and greedy
sultan who met a clever little cockerel...

Rapunzel

Jacqueline Wilson
Illustrated by Nick Sharratt

Once upon a time there was a baby who was
stolen by a witch...

Rumpelstiltskin

Kit Wright

Illustrated by Ted Dewan

Once upon a time there was a beautiful girl who
would die if she couldn't spin straw into gold...

The Three Heads
in the Well

Susan Gates

Illustrated by Sue Heap

Once upon a time there were two stepsisters —
one good, one bad — who both went out to seek
their fortunes...